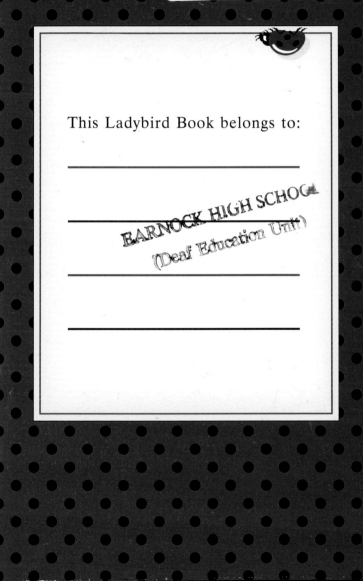

This Ladybird Book belongs to:

_____

EARNOCK HIGH SCHOOL
(Deaf Education Unit)

_____

_____

Ladybird

This Ladybird retelling
by
Audrey Daly

Ladybird books are widely available, but in case of
difficulty may be ordered by post or telephone from:

Ladybird Books – Cash Sales Department
Littlegate Road Paignton Devon TQ3 3BE
Telephone 0803 554761

A catalogue record for this book is available
from the British Library

First edition

Published by Ladybird Books Ltd Loughborough Leicestershire UK
Ladybird Books Inc Auburn Maine 04210 USA

Printed in England

FAVOURITE TALES

Tom
Thumb

illustrated
by
PETER STEVENSON

based on a story by Jacob and Wilhelm Grimm

There was once a woodsman and his wife who were very sad because they had no children.

"If only we had a child to love," said the wife, "I wouldn't mind if he were as small as my thumb!"

Time passed and at last they had a son, which made them both very happy.

Strangely enough, the boy never grew any bigger than a man's thumb, and so they called him "Tom Thumb".

One day, as Tom's father set off for work, he sighed, "If only Tom were bigger, he could drive the cart into the forest for me."

Tom looked at his mother. "I can do it anyway!" he said. "If you will harness the horse, Mother, I'll show you how." Tom's mother did as he asked.

"Now put me in the horse's ear," said Tom. "I'll tell him which way to go."

So off went the cart with Tom tucked in the horse's ear. When Tom said, "Turn left," or "Turn right," the horse did just that.

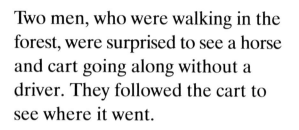

Two men, who were walking in the forest, were surprised to see a horse and cart going along without a driver. They followed the cart to see where it went.

When the cart stopped, the two men were amazed to see Tom's father lift him down from the horse's ear.

"What a clever little fellow that is," said one of the men. "Will you sell him to us?"

"I would never sell him," said the woodsman proudly. "He is my son."

But Tom whispered, "Go on, Father, let me go with them. It will be an adventure, and I know I can get home soon."

The woodsman didn't want to, but at last he sold Tom for a lot of money.

One of the men put Tom in his pocket, saying, "We can put him on show in the towns. He is going to make us rich!" Then they set off.

Towards evening, Tom called out, "Please put me down so that I can stretch my legs."

When the men put him down, Tom ran straight off and hid. The men looked everywhere, but he had disappeared.

Tom looked for somewhere safe
to sleep. He soon found an empty
snail shell and curled up inside it.
Just as he was falling asleep, he
heard voices nearby.

Two thieves were talking. "We'll
sneak into the parson's house and
steal his money!" said one.

"Take me with you," said Tom in a
loud voice. "I can help you!"

The men were puzzled. They could
hear a voice, but they couldn't see
anyone. They were astonished
when they found the tiny boy.

"I can get in through a crack in the window," said Tom, "and I can throw the money down to you."

The men agreed to take Tom with them and see what he could do.

When they got to the parson's house, Tom did as he had said. Then, standing on the window ledge, he shouted, "Do you want *all* the money that's here?"

"Sssh!" said the thieves, frightened. "You'll wake the whole house!"

But Tom shouted even louder.
"HOW MUCH MONEY
SHOULD I THROW DOWN?"

The noise woke the cook, who
was sleeping in the next room.

While the cook got up to look around, Tom ran off to the barn. There he settled down to sleep in the hay.

By the time the cook got downstairs, the thieves had run away and there was no sign of Tom at all.

Next morning the cook went to milk and feed the cow. She picked up the very bundle of hay that Tom was sleeping in.

Tom woke up to find himself being tossed up and down in the cow's mouth. He landed in the cow's stomach with all the hay.

"Stop eating!" yelled Tom. "I'm getting smothered!"

The cook was so startled to hear a voice coming from the cow's mouth that she ran to the parson. "Help!" she cried. "The cow's talking!"

"Don't be silly," said the parson.
"Cows don't talk."

Just then Tom shouted again – the
parson was astonished.

As soon as he could, Tom crawled
out of the cow's stomach and
slipped away. No one saw him go.

But Tom's troubles were far from
over. A hungry wolf was passing
by and saw Tom in the farmyard.

"This will make
a tasty little snack,"
thought the wolf, and he
swallowed Tom in one gulp.

Clever Tom quickly thought of a plan. "Wolf," he called, "if you are still hungry, I know where there is lots of food." And he told the wolf how to get to his very own house, which was not far away.

When they got there, Tom said, "Just crawl through the drain and you'll be in the kitchen, where there is always plenty to eat."

The drain was quite small, but the wolf squeezed and pushed and *just* managed to get through.

In the kitchen, the wolf ate so much that when he tried to crawl back through the drain, he was much too fat!

Then Tom began to shout and sing at the top of his voice.

His parents came to the kitchen door to see what all the noise was about.

"It's a wolf!" said Tom's father. "Where's my axe?"

"Wait, Father!" shouted Tom. "It's me! I'm here, inside the wolf's stomach!"

"Tom!" cried his father. "Don't worry, we'll save you!"

Tom's father picked up his axe and hit the wolf over the head. Then, very carefully, he cut a little hole in the wolf's stomach.

Out jumped Tom, safe and sound. "I told you I'd be back soon, Father!" he laughed.

Tom's parents were overjoyed to see him. "We'll never part with you again," said his father, "not for all the money in the world."

"And I will never leave home again," promised Tom. "I've had enough adventures to last a lifetime!"